TEN LITTLE DINOSAURS

MIKE BROWNLOW SIMON RICKERTY

Sandy Creek
NEW YORK

Ten little dinosaurs, hatching from their eggs,

Blinking in the sunshine, stretching out their legs.

"Look! Our mommy's sleeping. Let's go and explore!"

Ten little dinosaurs all say . . .

"Roarrrrr!"

Ten little dinosaurs, walking in a line.

10

"Stomp!"

goes Diplodocus.

Now there are . . .

. . . nine.

9

Nine little dinosaurs think the world smells great!

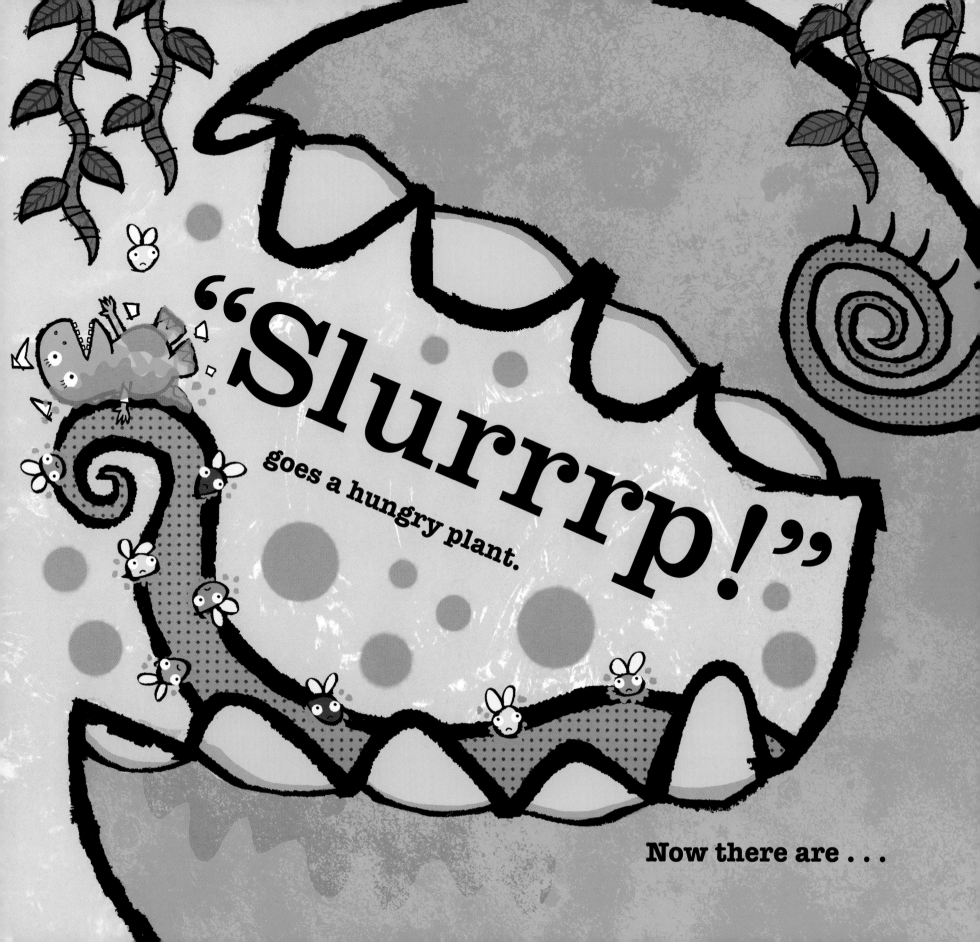

"Slurrrp!"

goes a hungry plant.

Now there are . . .

. . . **eight.**

8

**Eight little dinosaurs
peep inside a cavern.**

. . . **seven.**

Seven little dinosaurs
in a tricky fix.

7

"Caaaark!"

shrieks a pterosaur.

Now there are . . .

. . . **six.**

**Six little dinosaurs
need to duck and dive.**

6

. . . five.

Five little dinosaurs hear an angry roar.

Charge!

goes Triceratops.

5

Now there are . . .

...four.

Four little dinosaurs, wobbling on a tree.

Snap!

goes the plesiosaur.

Now there are . . .

4

. . . three.

**Three little dinosaurs,
trying to dodge the poo.**

3

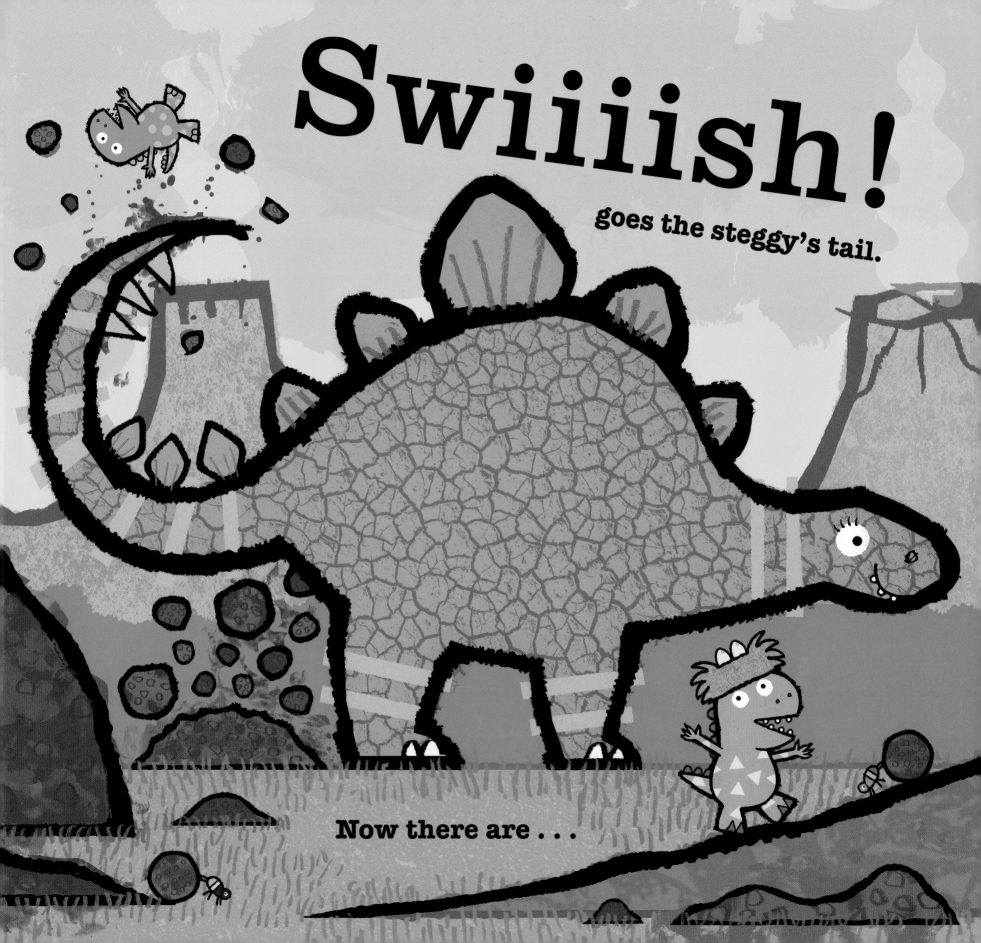

. . . two.

Two little dinosaurs—all the others gone.

2

One little dinosaur. Has he met his doom?
What's that scary creature
stomping through the gloom?

It's not a raptor, not a T-Rex,

not a monster . . . PHEW!

It's Mom who's come to find him . . .

and all the others, too!

Safe at home with Mommy—
who could ask for more?

For Toby
M.B.

For Erin & Isla
S.R.

An Imprint of Sterling Publishing
1166 Avenue of the Americas
New York, NY 10036

Text © 2015 by Mike Brownlow
Illustrations © 2015 by Simon Rickerty

First published in 2015 in Great Britain by Orchard Books, an imprint of Hachette Children's Group.

This 2015 edition published by Sandy Creek.

ISBN 978-1-4351-6155-9

Manufactured in China
Lot #:
2 4 6 8 10 9 7 5 3 1
05/15